THE INDIAN IN THE CUPBOARD

by
Lynne Reid Banks

Student Packet

Written by:
Gloria Levine, M.A.
Mary L. Dennis, Editor

Contains masters for:

3	Prereading Activities
1	Study Guide
4	Vocabulary Activities
2	Critical Thinking Activities
2	Literary Analysis Activities
3	Writing Activities
1	Review Crossword
2	Comprehension Quizzes (two levels)
2	Unit Exams (two levels)
	Detailed Answer Key

PLUS

Note
The text used to prepare this guide was the Avon Books softcover, copyright 1980 by Lynne Reid Banks. If other editions are used, page references may vary slightly.

ISBN 1-56137-693-0

To order, contact your local
school supply store, or—

Novel Units, Inc.
P.O. Box 791610
San Antonio, TX 78279

Name_____

Directions
Rate each of the following statements before you read the book. Discuss your ratings with a partner or in a small group.

1———-2———-3———-4———-5———-6
agree   disagree
strongly   strongly

1. I wouldn't want to know my future. _____

2. Revenge is sweet. _____

3. Forgive and forget. _____

4. There are some things adults don't need to know about. _____

5. A friend is someone who can keep a secret. _____

6. A friend is someone who forgives you when you make a mistake. _____

7. Native Americans never really scalped anyone. _____

8. Old westerns always show stereotypes of Native Americans— not the way they really were. _____

9. Native Americans lived in tepees _____

10. Native Americans introduced colonists to corn. _____

11. Native Americans introduced pioneers to horseback riding. _____

12. Today, movies and toys are accurate in the way they show Native Americans. _____

13. Talking about your anger is always better than using your fists. _____

14. I'd trust my best friend with a secret before I'd trust my brother or sister or mother or father. _____

Name_____

Directions
Read each of the situations below and mark the choice that best describes what YOU would do. **After reading the story,** mark the choice that describes what CHARACTERS IN THE STORY do.

1. Your best friend has just given you a cheap little thing for your birthday present—something you know he no longer wants himself. What would you do?
   (a) Say thank you but don't try to hide your disappointment.
   (b) Say thank you and pretend to like the gift.
   (c) Say exactly how you feel—that this is a ROTTEN present.
   (d) Say nothing at all but plan to give him or her an equally rotten present.

2. You discover that when you locked your plastic Indian in a certain cupboard, he became real! What would you do next?
   (a) Get all your plastic figures together and put them in the cupboard.
   (b) Pick up the Indian and try to play with him.
   (c) Get him some food and shelter.
   (d) Lock him back in the cupboard right away! This is too weird for you!

3. Whom would you tell about the toy-turned-real?
   (a) absolutely no one
   (b) only your best friend
   (c) your best friend and your parents
   (d) your best friend, your parents, and your brothers

4. The little live Indian is bleeding severely from a wound. What would you do?
   (a) Go to your mother or father for help.
   (b) Call 911.
   (c) Cut up tiny strips of bandage and apply them to the wound, using a magnifying glass to see what you're doing.
   (d) Put a plastic doctor in the cupboard so that he will come alive and be able to help the Indian.

Name_____

5. A store owner accuses your friend of shoplifting. You are with him and know that he hasn't done any such thing. What would you do?
    (a) Speak up and politely say that you've been with him the whole time and he hasn't taken a thing.
    (b) Tell the store owner angrily that he has a lot of nerve accusing your friend.
    (c) Keep quiet for fear that you will get in trouble, too.
    (d) Keep quiet because to tell the truth, you think it's pretty funny to see your friend in hot water.

6. You are a father, now. Something is missing from your workshop and you find that your son has taken it without asking you. What would you probably do?
    (a) angrily demand to know what he has done with it
    (b) lose your cool and tell him that he is grounded for a week
    (c) tell him calmly that you don't touch his things and he shouldn't touch yours
    (d) demand that he replace it, but respect his choice not to tell you where it is

Name_____

Indian in the Cupboard
Activity #3: Critical Thinking
Use Before Reading

Directions

Imagine that one morning you wake up and find that some of the plastic toys in your room have become real living people. Sounds great, huh? But think of all the problems that might pop up. For starters, the little people depend on you for everything they need to live. Where will you find these items? How will you get them to live together peaceably? How will you protect them from the dangers that surround them? What rules will you set up?

Jot down some notes below. Then read the story to see what steps Omri takes when he finds that two little people are depending on him.

Who Comes to Life:
   a Cowboy   an Indian   and _____
                                                                     (another plastic figure
                                                                      found in your room)

Food You Will Provide

Shelter You Will Provide

Household Items Your Little People Will Use (dishes, bathing, bedding, etc.)

Transportation Needed

Other Necessities:

Companionship

Safety

Entertainment

© Novel Units, Inc.

6

Name_____

Directions
Write a brief answer to each study question as you read the novel at home or in class. Use the questions for review before group discussions and before your novel test.

Chapters 1-2

1. List the birthday presents Omri receives—and the givers.

2. Why does Omri's mother ask him not to lose the key?

3. What is shown in the picture on page 8?

4. Why does Little Bear stab Omri's finger?

5. Why doesn't Omri tell Patrick about Little Bear right away?

6. After school, Omri feels sick and his mother puts him to bed. Why does Omri recover so quickly?

7. List the supplies Omri gathers for Little Bear—and their uses.

8. Omri explains what corn is by saying that it is like the food Little Bear has where he comes from. How is this "a shot in the dark"? (p.19)

9. Why do you think Omri loses his desire to handle Little Bear?

10. When Omri first sees Little Bear, he wishes one of his brothers or his father would come in, and later he is tempted to tell Patrick. Whom do you think he will tell—if anyone?

7

Chapters 3-4

1. Why does the tepee become real but not the Matchbox car?

2. Why isn't Little Bear as excited about the magic of the cupboard as Omri is?

3. How would Little Bear have reacted if Omri were French instead of English?

4. How does Omri answer Little Bear's request for weapons?

5. Why does Little Bear want to go outside?

6. Outdoors, how does Little Bear show that he is brave but not reckless?

7. How does Omri begin to see things from Little Bear's point of view?

8. Why does Omri bring back Tommy?

9. How can you tell that Omri is not thinking ahead when he brings back Tommy?

10. Will Tommy be willing and able to do what Omri wants? What will Omri do with Tommy, now that Tommy is real?

Chapters 5-6

1. How does Omri convince Tommy not to be frightened?

2. Why does Omri send Tommy back to the war?

3. List the items Omri gets for Little Bear in this section—and why.

4. Why does Omri make the knight real?

5. Why does Omri think about the Saracens as he puts the knight back in the cupboard? (Research the answer.)

6. How does Omri break the rules at lunchtime—and why?

7. When you're interested in learning something, the learning often comes easier. Find two examples of this in the story.

8. Explain why this chapter is called, "The Chief is Dead, Long Live the Chief."

9. How can you tell that Omri's father has a quick temper, but doesn't pry into his children's secrets?

10. Omri is having a hard time saying no to Little Bear. What else do you think Omri will do for Little Bear?

Chapters 7-8

1. Why does Omri show Little Bear to Patrick?

2. How does Patrick help Omri solve the problem of getting a fire for Little Bear to cook over?

3. What happens before and after what is shown on page 66?

4. How does Omri convince Patrick not to put dozens of plastic people into the cupboard?

5. How does Omri use a piece of his Erector set to solve a problem?

6. Why doesn't Little Bear eat the meat he cooked and what does he eat instead?

7. When Patrick gets shot, why does Omri tell him it serves him right?

8. How does Omri convince Patrick to leave the cowboy at Omri's?

9. How does Patrick convince Omri to take the cowboy and Indian to school the next day?

10. What problems do you think will arise when Omri takes the cowboy and Indian to school?

© Novel Units, Inc.

10

Chapters 9-10

1. Why does the cowboy call Omri a "hallucy-nation" and start crying?

2. Why does Omri put the cowboy and his horse into a crate overnight—and how does the cowboy escape?

3. Why does Little Bear want to kill the cowboy?

4. How did the cowboy get his nickname?

5. Why does Omri take Little Bear to Yapp's?

6. How does Omri get the two little men to eat breakfast together?

7. What is on the spoon in the picture on page 100?

8. When Omri offers the two breakfast, who seems more appreciative, Little Bear or Boone?

9. After breakfast, why do you think Omri lets Little Bear and Boone fight?

10. Will Little Bear and Boone get along better in the future?

Chapters 11-12

1. Why does Omri fill an eggcup full of water—and who seems happiest to see it?

2. Why are the members of Omri's family so grumpy at breakfast?

3. Why doesn't Omri act on his impulse to "bash" April and the other kids who are teasing him?

4. Why does Little Bear stab Omri through his pocket?

5. Why does Mr. Johnson yell at Omri?

6. Why does Omri put Little Bear and Boone into the same pocket?

7. At lunchtime, why does Omri give both little men to Patrick?

8. Why is Patrick late to Miss Hilton's class and what is the consequence?

9. How do you explain Patrick's strange behavior in Mr. Johnson's office?

10. Why do you think the headmaster's face is white when he comes out of his office with Patrick? What do you think the headmaster will do now?

12

Chapters 13-14

1. Why has Patrick told the headmaster about the little men?

2. Why does Little Bear say that Boone's picture doesn't look like a real place?

3. How does Omri lie to his art teacher—and why?

4. How does Little Bear decide which plastic woman he wants Omri to buy?

5. Why does Mr. Yapp accuse Omri of stealing—then apologize?

6. Why does Adiel punch Omri—then stop and act embarrassed?

7. Why do Patrick and Omri clean up the attic?

8. Why does Little Bear shoot Boone?

9. How does Little Bear show that he is sorry that he injured Boone?

10. Who do you think will find the key? Where? How will it be used?

13

Chapters 15-16

1. Why do Patrick and Omri stay up all night?

2. Why do the boys put Boone's bed and Little Bear's seed box up onto the bedside table?

3. How does Omri figure out where the key is?

4. Does Little Bear know the dangers involved in looking for the key? Would he do it if he knew about the rat?

5. What does Tommy do for Boone that the boys can't?

6. Why does Little Bear get angry with Boone again as soon as Boone becomes conscious?

7. Why does Omri hide under the covers after putting the Indian woman in the cupboard?

8. Why do Omri and Patrick steal whisky from Omri's parents?

9. What sort of ceremony do Boone, Little Bear and Bright Eyes have with the boys before being sent back to their own time?

10. Why do you think the boys send back the little people? How can you tell that the boys have mixed feelings?

compost 1	shaft 7	coherent 7	baffled 10
minuscule 11	bandolier 11	intricate 11	fumbling 12
tantalizing 13	unwarily 13	appalled 15	falteringly 17
gaped 17	surveyed 18	longhouse 21	uncompromisingly 28
commando 28	stability 28	transported 28	lithely 28
ventured 29	ransacked 30	seething 31	brandishing 33
pommel 33	escarpment 39	cowering 39	foreboding 41

Directions
Use words from the vocabulary box to complete the analogies, below. Explain to a partner how you arrived at your answers.

SAMPLE: NO is to YES as _____ is to GIGANTIC   *(Answer: MINUSCULE)*

1.   BALANCE is to _____ as FALL OFF is to DISEQUILIBRIUM.

2.   TEPEE is to SIOUX as _____ is to IROQUOIS.

3.   GREEN BERET (SOLDIER) is to VIETNAM as_____ is to WW II.

4.   ROTTING GARBAGE is to REPULSIVE as BREAD BAKING is to

      _____.

5.   DUNE is to SAND as _____ is to DEAD LEAVES.

6.   HILL is to MOUNTAIN as SLOPE is to _____.

7.   HANDLE is to BRIEFCASE as _____ is to SADDLE.

8.   AWAKE is to ASLEEP as CAUTIOUSLY is to _____.

9.   STEEL is to RUBBER as _____is to COMPLIANTLY.

10.   HAUNTING MEMORY is to PAST as _____ is to FUTURE.

Name_____

Directions

Form a group of three. Cut up each set of cards, below. Then pick a card and read the clue on it to the others in your group. Together, figure out the mystery words. Individually, use each word in a sentence and draw or find a picture that shows what each word means.

Set #1:

This noun has two syllables, five letters.	The name for this jacket comes from the Aleut/Russian word for "pelt."	You should wear one on your next trip to the Arctic.

Set #2:

This noun has one syllable, five letters.		AKA "corn"

Set #3:

This noun has three syllables, eight letters.	The name for this ax is an Algonquin word.	A tool or weapon with both a boy's and a bird's name in it.

Set #4:

This verb has three syllables, ten letters.	startled into sudden activity	named after an Italian who studied electricity

Set #5:

This adverb has five syllables, 13 letters.	from the Latin for "big + soul" (unspitefully)	How you behave toward your enemies if you feel generous.

Name_____

Directions
Answer each question by circling the letter in the YES or NO space.

		YES	NO
1.	Would you probably hear **raucous** voices at a wild party?	L	N
2.	If you keep cool under pressure, are you **nonplussed?**	U	I
3.	Is a **bandolier** something you might play tunes on under the stars at night?	C	T
4.	Is a **persecutor** the opposite of the lawyer for the defense?	Y	E
5.	Is picking up glass fragments something you would do **gingerly?**	B	F
6.	Does a woman usually use her arms when she is **gesticulating?**	A	G
7.	Is a child who refuses to eat her peas being **mulish?**	R	H
8.	Is a person who whistles **dolefully** probably happy?	P	S
9.	Is a man who speaks **smugly** acting pretty sure of himself?	D	J
10.	Would you keep fresh water in a **quiver?**	K	O
11.	Is an **alcove** a body of water?	W	M

Question
What did Patrick tell the headmaster?
Fill in the letters that correspond to the numbered questions to find the answer.

$\overline{}\ \overline{}\ \overline{}\ \overline{}\ \overline{}\ \overline{}\ \ \ \overline{}\ \overline{}\ \overline{}\ \overline{}\ \ \overline{}\ \overline{}\ \overline{}\ \overline{}\ \overline{}\ \overline{}\ \overline{}$
  1   2   3   3   1   4   5   4   6   7   8   3   6   5   5   4   9

$\overline{}\ \overline{}\ \overline{}\ \overline{}.$
10 11   7   2

Name_____

Indian in the Cupboard
Activity #8: **Vocabulary**
Chapters 13-16

Directions

For each vocabulary word (followed by its page number), you are given the first letter of a synonym (word that means the same) and the first letter of an antonym (word that means the opposite). Work with a partner to complete the chart. (Use both a thesaurus and a dictionary, if you like.) In some cases, there is more than one correct answer.

Vocabulary Word	Synonym	Antonym
1. flummoxed (128)	B_____	U_____
2. infinite (128)	B_____	L_____
3. stonily (129)	P_____	K_____
4. enthralled (131)	M_____	B_____
5. infinitesimal (134)	M_____	I_____
6. hullabaloo (148)	U_____	L_____
7. restive (148)	I_____	R_____
8. bemused (176)	D_____	A_____
9. omnivorous (160)	M_____	V_____
10. bedraggled (162)	S_____	I_____
11. petered (181)	D_____	G_____

Name_____

Directions
Imagine that the magic cupboard is yours for a day. Write your own story about what happens when you put a plastic figure in the cupboard.

1. **Prewriting**
   Jot down ideas using the following chart:

What figure did you choose—and why?	What was your first meeting like?	Did you share your secret?

Your story idea: (Summarize in 3-4 sentences.)

_____

_____

_____

_____

What did you learn about the little person's world?	What problems did living in a giant's world present?	Why did/didn't the person want to return to his or her world?

2. **During writing**
   Use your notes to write your story. Make sure that you read your first draft aloud to a partner for comments before you revise it.

3. **After writing**
   Use brown construction paper to help your teacher make the bulletin board look like a huge cupboard. Display your compositions on different "shelves." Post the title, *The Indian in the Cupboard,* on a large paper key at the top of the display.

List poems consist of a list of things or events. They can be long or short, rhymed or unrhymed. List poems have been around for a long time. For an example, read Walt Whitman's "Leaves of Grass." Your PROJECT is to write a list poem about the items Omri collects for Little Bear.

Prewriting
1. In a small group, brainstorm a list of things Little Bear asks for and the things Omri gets for him. (One member of the group writes down the list.)
2. Brainstorm other items Omri might have taken to Little Bear, but did not.
3. As one person reads the list of items, close your eyes and imagine each one. What does it look and feel like? Where do you find it? What does it make you think of?
4. Jot down notes on each item. Is it hard to get? What is Little Bear's reaction to it? Where does he want it placed? What does Little Bear use it for? Does he change it or add to it? What problem does it solve? Does it create any new problems?
5. Decide the speaker in your poem. Will it be an observer or Omri—or even Little Bear? Why is the speaker making this list? Is it to help him remember things? Is it his reminder to someone else? Is it a list of complaints? Is it a list he made in a private diary, to keep a record of the wonderful things that have been happening? Is it a list made in answer to a question?

During Writing
6. Draft your list poem. Experiment with different beginnings. Are you going to start right away with the list—or tell why you are making the list and what it means? As you create images, think about connections between the items and try changing their order. Consider ending your poem with a one or two-line "surprise." (For example, you might not tell until the end who these things are for—or how Omri feels about collecting them.)
7. Write a second draft of your poem. Make sure that you "show" your reader each item (by using descriptive adjectives, metaphors, etc.)
8. Read the poem aloud and revise it. Play with sounds (like rhyming end words or putting together several words that start with the same sound). Try different ways of breaking up the lines until you get the one that "sounds right."

After Writing
9. Read your poem aloud and create a drawing, collage, or mobile to illustrate it.
10. Collect your group's poems and bind them into a booklet to be kept at a literature station (where it might tempt others to read the book).

Directions
Sometimes people act out of concern for others. Sometimes they are motivated by self-interest. Sometimes people are driven by both. Consider the following incidents in the story. Label an incident **S** if Omri is thinking about himself. Label an incident **E** if Omri is showing concern for someone else. (You may decide to label an incident both S and E.)

_____ 1.   Omri tells Patrick he likes the gift.

_____ 2.   After discovering the cupboard's secret, Omri thinks about putting lots of plastic figures inside.

_____ 3.   Omri decides not to tell anyone about the cupboard.

_____ 4.   Omri picks up Little Bear after being stabbed by him.

_____ 5.   Omri brings the old chief to life.

_____ 6.   Omri swipes small bits of food and his father's seed tray.

_____ 7.   Omri wrestles with Patrick and refuses to let him put any figures in the cupboard.

_____ 8.   Omri takes the little men to school.

_____ 9.   Omri has a fistfight with Patrick in the headmaster's office.

_____10.   Omri shows his art teacher Boone's drawing.

_____11.   Omri buys a plastic Indian woman.

_____12.   Omri discovers that the cupboard is missing and angrily flings things around Adiel's room.

_____13.   Omri puts the medic in the cupboard.

_____14.   Omri hides under the covers after putting the Indian woman in the cupboard.

_____15.   Omri let Little Bear prick Omri's finger before going back.

_____16.   Omri nearly couldn't bring himself to send Boone and the others back.

_____17.   Omri decided not to put medicine bottles in the cupboard and pretend that it was a doctor's drug cupboard.

Culminating Essay
Why does Omri give his mother the key at the end of the story? Has he changed since he first used it? Use incidents from the story, such as those above, to support your answer.

Name_____

Directions

With a partner, discuss Omri's decision to take Little Bear and Boone to school. Take turns jotting reasons why he should/should not have taken Little Bear and Boone in the YES and NO columns. It is okay to write down key words and phrases rather than whole sentences. Try to include as many reasons under "YES" as you do under "NO." Discuss your charts with another pair of partners and try to reach consensus (agreement) on whether or not Omri made the best decision. A spokesperson for this group of four then reports the group-of-four's conclusion to the whole class. Dissenting views are heard at this time.

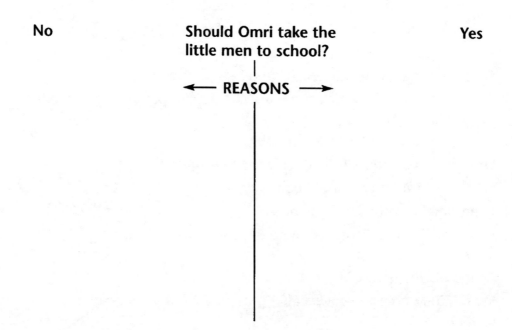

Conclusion

The reason that **best** supports the group's conclusion is:

On a separate sheet of paper, write an essay in which you tell whether you think Omri was right or wrong to take the little men to school.

Name_____

Directions

With a partner, think of words and phrases that describe Omri and put them in the box beneath his name. Then think of words and phrases that tell how Omri feels about the other characters and how each of them feels about him. Label the arrows with these words and phrases.

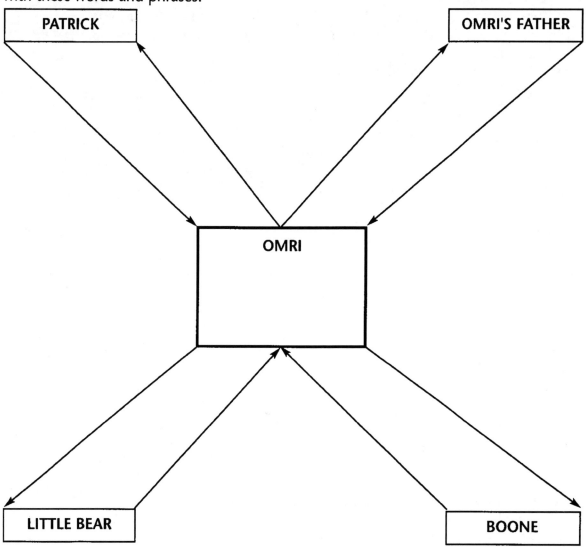

Essay

A character sketch is a brief, vivid description of a person. It includes physical characteristics—appearance, surroundings—and personality. Use the notes you have taken on the chart, above to write a character sketch of Omri.

Directions

Two steps in problem solving are: (a) brainstorming possible solutions and (b) judging how good each one is. When Little Bear shoots Boone with the arrow, Omri faces a problem. *What can he do for Boone, now that the key to the cupboard is missing?* Help Omri solve the problem by

a) Considering the choices in the chart below. (Add an idea of your own.)
b) Thinking about the criteria ("yardstick" questions used to measure how well a particular decision "measures up" by being useful), and
c) Scoring each decision: 1=yes, 2=maybe, or 3=no.

		Criteria:		
Possible Choices ↓	Will Boone recover?	Will this keep me out of trouble?	Will the secret remain a secret?	Will this keep others out of danger?
do nothing				
tell my parents				
send Little Bear to look for the key				

Which choice do you think is the best one? Why?

On another sheet of paper, write the story that tells what happens when Omri makes a decision different from the one he made in the novel.

Name_____

Indian in the Cupboard
Activity #15: **Reader Response**
Use After Reading

Part I

When Patrick demanded that Omri give him both little men at school, Omri realized that even nice people can get mean when they are determined to get something they want. Describe someone you once saw turn mean. First, jot down ideas in the chart below.

Who was the person, and what are they usually like?	What did the person want, and why?	What was frustrating the person?

Summary of your story:

_____

_____

_____

_____

How did the person's behavior affect you?	Did the person get what he or she wanted?	How did the person react to the outcome of the situation?

Part II

After Patrick showed the little men to the headmaster, Omri felt as if his friendship with Patrick was being destroyed. Describe a serious disagreement you once had with your best friend. Use a chart like the one above to jot answers to questions you want to answer in your essay and to write a summary. Then write the essay.

© Novel Units, Inc.

25

All rights reserved

Crossword Puzzle

ACROSS

2. shelter built by Little Bear
4. Omri takes Gillon's magnifying

   _____.
6. Boone and Little Bear become ___ brothers.
8. Omri's father's hobby.
9. Little Bear wears a ___cloth.
10. Little Bear is almost killed by Gillon's

    _____.
11. Omri says the whinnying sound is his windup_____.
13. Little Bear is a member of this tribe.
14. They were enemies of Little Bear's tribe.
15. The main foods of the Iroquois were called the three _____.
22. Boone makes one of his hometown.
23. The shopkeeper accuses Omri of this.
24. Omri brings him to life to get an ax for Little Bear.
25. Little Bear and Boone have very different reactions when watching this on TV.
28. Iroquois Indians were sometimes called the _____ Nations.
32. Little Bear is _____ inches high.
33. He thinks he is drunk when he wakes up in a world of giants.
34. Toffo is a brand name for a type of English _____.

DOWN

1. The old cupboard is a present from him.
3. Little Bear takes this from the dead chief.
5. Omri is not much of one.
7. He discovers that having little people is a big responsibility.
12. He goes home for a "rest" after seeing Little Bear and Boone in his office at school.
16. Omri is a good one.
17. the author of the novel
18. British word for the game of soccer.
19. The main foods of the Iroquois were squash, beans, and _____.
20. Omri's art teacher is amazed that his drawing is so _____.
21. British word for cookies.
26. Omri is horrified to learn that Little Bear took 30 of these from the French.
27. Little Bear crawls under the floorboards looking for this.
29. Little Bear shoots Boone with one.
30. Tommy's occupation.
31. British word for a truck or van.

Name_____

True/False
Mark each statement **T** or **F**. Briefly explain why the false statements are incorrect.

___1.   Omri received the cabinet as a birthday present from his friend Patrick.
___2.   Omri was delighted by the toy Indian his brother Gillon gave him for his birthday.
___3.   When Omri locked the toy Indian in the cupboard with his great-grand mother's key, the Indian became real.
___4.   When Omri put objects into the cabinet, only the metal ones became real.
___5.   Little Bear demanded to have a tepee instead of a longhouse.
___6.   The horse kicked Little Bear because of Omri.
___7.   Omri made a toy medic real so that the medical supplies in the medic's bag could be used to treat Little Bear's injury.
___8.   Omri made the toy knight real so that Little Bear would have a companion.
___9.   When Omri brought an old chief to life, Little Bear fought and killed the chief.
___10. When Omri's father discovered that he had taken the seed tray, he yelled at Omri and grounded him for a week.
___11. Omri decided that he could trust his two brothers with his secret.
___12. Omri gave paint to Little Bear, who used it as warpaint on his face.
___13. When Patrick found out about the magic of the cupboard, he demanded to have his own little person.
___14. Patrick was shot by a cowboy's gun when he brought the toy man to life.
___15. Omri decided to bring the tiny men to school so that he and Patrick could play with them at recess.

Causes

___16. Omri said that he wished his cupboard locked.

___17. Little Bear grew angry when Omri reached into the cupboard to touch him.

___18. Omri locked Little Bear back in the cupboard.

___19. Little Bear said that it was no good to ride the horse on a blanket.

___20. Gillon lost his rat.

Effects

A. Omri's finger was pierced by a little knife.

B. Little Bear became plastic again.

C. He shot Omri with a tiny gun.

D. Omri's father went to his workshop and made Omri a key.

E. Omri decided to take Little Bear outside.

F. He went to Omri's room and saw the longhouse.

G. Omri's mother let him have a keepsake her grandmother gave her

---

Completion
Fill in each blank with the word or phrase that makes the statement true.

When Omri's brother gives him an old 1._____ as a birthday present, Omri

puts a plastic 2._____ in it and locks it with a key that had once

belonged to his 3._____. The next morning, Omri is amazed to

discover that 4._____. Omri begins

secretly collecting supplies for Little Bear, such as birch bark and twigs for him to

make into a 5._____. When the horse Omri has gotten for Little Bear

kicks the tiny man, Omri brings Tommy, a 6._____ to life and Tommy

treats Little Bear's wound. Omri also brings back two other men, a(n)

7._____ and a(n) 8._____, so that he can

remove some of their things for Little Bear's use. From them, Little Bear ends up with

a(n) 9._____ and a (n) 10._____. Shortly after Omri

brings the second little man to life, the man 11._____. Omri is shocked, but

Little Bear calmly proclaims that 12._____.

When Omri decides to let his best friend, Patrick, in on the secret, Patrick insists on

bringing Boone, a 13._____, to life. Omri doesn't think it is a

good idea to 14._____, but he agrees to do so when

Patrick threatens to 15._____, otherwise.

Short Answer
Answer each question in a complete sentence.

16. Why did some things become real when put in the cupboard, but not others?

17. Explain how Little Bear ends up with a paintbrush, a tiny cup, and a small blanket.

18. How is Patrick different from Omri in the way they treat the tiny men?

19. Why doesn't Omri tell his family about the secret of the cupboard?

20. How and why do both Little Bear and Boone hurt the boys when the plastic figures first became real?

Identification
Find a character in the box who matches the description on the left. Write the letter of the character next to the matching number. Each character is to be used only once.

___ 1. He respected his children's right to have secrets.

___ 2. She wore the key to her grandmother's jewel box around her neck for a long time.

___ 3. He blurted out the secret to the headmaster.

___ 4. He was accused of shoplifting while looking for a plastic Indian woman.

___ 5. Omri's oldest brother, he hid the cabinet and lost the key.

___ 6. He was the medic who treated both Little Bear and Boone.

___ 7. Patrick chose to bring this plastic cowboy to life.

___ 8. An Iroquois, he was not used to riding horses.

___ 9. His allowance had been cut off, so he gave Omri a used cupboard for a birthday present.

> A. Omri
> B. Patrick
> C. Gillon
> D. Omri's father
> E. Omri's mother
> F. Little Bear
> G. Tommy
> H. Boone
> I. Adiel

Multiple Choice
To the left of each item number, write the number of the BEST response.

___ 10. Which of the following does NOT describe Omri?
  a. generally pretty messy
  b. likes arranging things in drawers
  c. good speller
  d. not much interested in reading

___ 11. The more time Omri spent with Little Bear and Boone, the more he
  a. wished he had never turned the magic key in the cupboard lock
  b. felt like playing with them as if they were wind-up toys
  c. wondered whether he should tell his parents about them
  d. realized what a responsibility it was to be in charge of living people

___ 12. When the Indian chief died shortly after being brought to life in the cupboard, Little Bear acted
    a. matter-of-fact, unbothered
    b. moved, saddened
    c. puzzled, curious
    d. upset, angry

___ 13. Boone nearly died when
    a. a bird attacked him
    b. he fell from a bookshelf
    c. Gillon's rat bit him
    d. Little Bear shot him with an arrow

___ 14. Little Bear risked his life to save Boone by
    a. drawing the rat's attention from Boone to himself
    b. searching for the key while the rat was loose
    c. jumping into the bathtub to save Boone
    d. climbing into the lighted stove to save Boone

___ 15. Patrick showed that he was willing to stick up for his friend by telling
    a. the headmaster Omri was no troublemaker
    b. the shopkeeper Omri was no shoplifter
    c. Little Bear Omri was not his servant
    d. Gillon to stop picking on Omri

___ 16. Which was NOT a problem faced by Omri in this book?
    a. how to keep Little Bear from hurting Gillon's pet rat
    b. how to keep Patrick from revealing the secret
    c. how to keep Little Bear and Boone from hurting each other
    d. how to find a wife for Little Bear

___ 17. Which of the following is NOT something Lynn Reid Banks needed to know about in order to write this story?
    a. the French and Indian wars
    b. the shelters built by the Iroquois
    c. songs cowboys used to sing while driving cattle
    d. what brothers sound like when they argue

___ 18. Omri told his brothers there was a pony under his bed
    a. to make them laugh
    b. so that they wouldn't suspect that it was true
    c. so that they would look
    d. so that they would think he was crazy

___ 19. If Omri hadn't been able to bring Tommy to life,
    a. Tommy would have been killed in World War I
    b. Patrick might not have believed that the cupboard was magic
    c. the Germans might not have been defeated in World War I
    d. Little Bear might have died

___ 20. When Boone found himself in Omri's world, he assumed that
    a. Omri was the inventor of a time machine
    b. he (Boone) had died and gone to heaven
    c. Omri was some sort of magician
    d. he (Boone) was under the influence of alcohol

___ 21. Boone didn't like his nickname. Omri understood how he felt, because kids used to
    a. tease him about his crying
    b. call him "Omnibus"
    c. tease him about all the books he read
    d. call him "Ornery"

___ 22. You can tell that Omri sometimes believed in getting revenge. He was seeking revenge when he
    a. gave Gillon a broken box for his birthday
    b. hid Adiel's prized possessions
    c. took gardening supplies from his father
    d. sneaked food from the kitchen

___ 23. You can tell that Omri sometimes used physical violence to solve a problem. Evidence for this is what happened in the story when Omri
    a. was taunted by other kids at school
    b. was stabbed through the pocket by Little Bear
    c. thought that Patrick was going to tell the headmaster about Little Bear and Boone
    d. found Little Bear and Boone shooting at each other

____ 24. One of the reasons Omri decided to take Little Bear outside of the house was so that
  a. his mother wouldn't find Little Bear when she cleaned
  b. Little Bear could help choose a wife
  c. Little Bear could hunt ants
  d. Patrick and he could play with Little Bear in the park

____ 25. When the two men came out of Patrick's pocket at school they were
  a. both unconscious
  b. having a fistfight
  c. hugging because they were terrified
  d. plastic once more

____ 26. Patrick helped Omri solve the problem of
  a. getting Boone and Little Bear to eat together
  b. getting Boone to stop drinking so much
  c. keeping Little Bear hidden from Mr. Johnson
  d. making a fire for Little Bear

____ 27. When Omri brought in an eggcup full of water,
  a. Boone said that he didn't eat boiled eggs
  b. Little Bear quickly led his horse over to drink
  c. Little Bear was more eager to take a bath than Boone
  d. Boone was more eager to wash his clothes than Little Bear

____ 28. Little Bear stabbed Omri through his pocket because
  a. Little Bear was bored
  b. Little Bear was trying to make an airhole
  c. Little Bear accidentally dropped his ax
  d. Little Bear thought he was stabbing Boone

____ 29. Omri punched Patrick in Mr. Johnson's office because
  a. Omri didn't want Mr. Johnson to suspect that he planned the theft with his friend
  b. Omri wanted to draw Mr. Johnson's attention away from what was happening under the desk
  c. Patrick said that Omri made him late to class
  d. Patrick started to show the headmaster Little Bear

___ 30. When Boone drew a picture of his hometown, Omri
    A. hid it in his locker
    B. showed it to his art teacher
    C. gave it to his mother as a present
    D. glued it to the head of a pin

___ 31. Adiel punched Omri because
    A. Omri had switched the channel on TV to watch a western
    B. Omri had taken his plastic Indian
    C. Adiel thought Omri had stolen his magnifying glass
    D. Adiel thought Omri had taken his shorts

___ 32. Little Bear shot Boone with an arrow because
    A. Boone was cheering on the cowboys against the Indians on TV
    B. Boone had just fired a shot at Little Bear with his rifle
    C. Boone had threatened to build a saloon next to Little Bear's longhouse
    D. Boone refused to let Little Bear try on his hat

___ 33. Little Bear went under the floorboards because
    A. Omri figured that the key had fallen there
    B. Omri's father was about to pull them up and look for the rat
    C. Omri's mother had come into the room with a vacuum cleaner
    D. Little Bear was looking for an underground stream for fishing

___ 34. Tommy didn't give Boone penicillin because
    A. Tommy didn't want Boone to recover
    B. penicillin hadn't been discovered yet
    C. Boone was allergic to penicillin
    D. Boone refused to take the penicillin

___ 35. Little Bear said he hadn't heard of the "Indian custom" of becoming a blood brother because
    A. it was a secret custom the Iroquois were not supposed to reveal to outsiders
    B. it was a custom among the Algonquins, not the Iroquois
    C. it wasn't really a custom that started with the Indians
    D. he was embarrassed by the custom and pretended not to know of it

___ 36. Omri stole whiskey from his father's liquor cabinet because
    A. Patrick dared him to
    B. Omri needed to empty the cabinet so he could use it
    C. Omri needed it to make a special cake for Little Bear's wedding
    D. Boone needed the whiskey for medicinal purposes

___ 37. When Little Bear first looked at Bright Eyes
    A. she screamed and fainted
    B. she hid from him
    C. he was amazed and pleased to see her
    D. he was disappointed that she was not Iroquois

___ 38. When angry with Patrick or Little Bear or Boone, Omri sometimes used the same tone of voice with them as _____.
    A. they used with him
    B. his brothers used with him
    C. his parents and teachers used with him
    D. he used when scolding his dog

___39. After sending the little people back to their own times, the boys decided to
_____
    A. tell Omri's mother what had happened
    B. leave the cupboard empty in case they decide to bring their friends back
    C. burn the cupboard
    D. bring back Little Bear and Boone on Omri's birthday every year

___40. In telling a friend about this novel, you would most likely describe it as
    A. sentimental and melodramatic
    B. filled with suspense, action, and humor
    C. a riveting whodunit
    D. a modern Western novel

Use separate paper for the answers to this test. Be sure you identify each section on your answer pages.

Identification
Explain who each character is and briefly describe him or her in one or two sentences.

1. Omri
2. Patrick
3. Gillon
4. Omri's father
5. Omri's mother
6. Little Bear
7. Tommy
8. Boone
9. Adiel

Short Answer
Answer each question in one or two complete sentences.

10. Describe the incident in the story that was most suspenseful for you.
11. Tell when you would most like to have been one of the characters in the story.
12. Name one thing you would like about being a member of Omri's family—and one thing you wouldn't.
13. Name one thing you would like about having Patrick for a best friend—and one thing you wouldn't.
14. Why did Omri decide to bring Little Bear and Boone to school? What are two other choices he had?
15. Do you think Omri should have told Patrick about the cupboard?
16. Explain how Omri and Patrick both ended up in the headmaster's office.
17. How can you tell that both Little Bear and Boone enjoyed doing artwork?
18. Much has been said about the impact of TV violence on viewers. How did watching violence on TV affect Little Bear and Boone in the story?
19. How did Little Bear risk his life to save Boone—and why?

© Novel Units, Inc.

37

Essay

I. Creative Writing: Choose either A or B.
  A. Omri and Patrick have taken a walk after sending Little Bear and the others back. Patrick has finally gone home and now Omri is thinking aloud about the events of the past few days. Write down his thoughts.
  B. Pretend that you are Little Bear or Boone. Describe your recent experiences with time travel.

II. Analysis: Choose either A or B. Your essay should consist of at least three paragraphs. Make sure that your ideas are supported with reasons, evidence, examples, and details.
  A. How does Omri change as a result of his experience with the cupboard? What has he learned?
  B. Compare and contrast Patrick and Omri. What do they have in common? How are they different? Why do you think they are friends?

III. Evaluative Writing: Choose either A or B. Make sure that you support your opinion with plenty of evidence from the story and from your personal experience and reading. Your essay should not only develop your opinion, but consider other sides of the issue.
  A. Do you think that Omri was right to keep his discovery secret from his mother, father, and brothers?
  B. Do you think that Omri should have sent Little Bear back and stopped using the cupboard as soon as he realized its power?

IV. Personal essay: Choose A or B.
  A. Describe a secret you once shared with only your best friend.
  B. Describe a time when you realized how wrong a particular stereotype was as you got to know someone.

Answer Key

Activities #1, #2, and #3: Allow students time to discuss their answers to open-ended activities such as these—as a class, in groups, or with partners.

Study Questions

Chapters 1-2

1. plastic Indian-Patrick; skateboard-parents; helmet-Adiel; cupboard-Gillon
2. It was a gift from her dying grandmother, the key to her grandmother's jewel box.
3. Omri opens the cupboard the morning after his birthday and finds that the plastic Indian he locked inside has become real.
4. When Omri reaches in to touch the frightened Indian, he attacks.
5. He wants to keep the wonderful secret to himself, for a while, and thinks Patrick wouldn't believe him anyway.
6. Omri is upset when he finds that the Indian has become plastic again. Omri is happy when he finds that the Indian is real again, after his mother leaves the room.
7. small circle of paper plate-plate for Little Bear; corn, bread, cheese, corned beef, Coke-food for Little Bear; pick-up sticks, string, handkerchief, bit of felt-tepee for shelter; piece from a sweater-blanket
8. Omri doesn't really know where Little Bear comes from, and is probing with his comments and questions to see if his suspicions are correct.
9. Omri realizes that Little Bear is a real human being whose dignity ought to be respected.

Chapters 3-4

1. When the key is used to lock the cupboard, only plastic objects become real; the Matchbox car is metal.
2. Because of traditional belief, Little Bear is used to the idea of the spirits working magic.
3. Little Bear's tribe were enemies of the French, so Little Bear probably would have been much more distrustful of Omri.
4. Omri refuses to get Little Bear a gun, but promises to make him a bow and arrows.
5. He has difficulty riding his horse on the carpet.
6. He rides his horse, bravely facing ants and birds, but soon rides back to Omri and asks for weapons.
7. He realizes that little stones are like boulders to Little Bear and the edge of the lawn is like a cliff.
8. Omri needs to get at the things in Tommy's medical bag to treat Little Bear, who has been kicked by the horse.
9. Omri doesn't think about the fact that the medic will become real, as well as his bag.

Chapters 5-6

1. Omri tells Tommy that he is having a dream and that he'll soon wake up.
2. Tommy wants to go back to help win the war.

---

3. twigs, bark-to make a longhouse; grass-horse
4. Omri takes the ax from the knight for Little Bear's use.
5. Omri tells himself not to feel sorry for the knight, who looks as vicious as the knights during the Middle Ages must have looked when they were killing Saracens (Muslims).
6. Although students aren't supposed to leave the school grounds at lunchtime unless eating at home, Omri goes to the store to buy another Indian.
7. Omri wants to learn about the Iroquois, so becomes interested in the book although he isn't usually much of a reader. Usually bored by sewing, he gets immersed in sewing the tepee for Little Bear.
8. When Little Bear brings an old chief to life, the chief dies and Little Bear proclaims himself chief.
9. He yells when he finds that his seed box is missing, but doesn't press Omri about what he has done with it.

Chapters 7-8
1. Omri wants to tell someone, and thinks that if he doesn't share the secret with Patrick, their friendship will be over.
2. Patrick suggests using a little tar and putting twigs on top to make it look like a campfire.
3. Omri discovers that Gillon and Adiel have gone into his room to search for Gillon's rat; they are marveling over the longhouse. Omri tells them to leave as the tiny horse starts whinnying under the bed.
4. Omri grabs him and tries to explain that the people would be real and would do what they wanted to.
5. He makes a tiny spit for roasting meat with a piece of his Erector set.
6. The meat is squashed underfoot during a scuffle between Patrick and Omri; instead, Omri gets him some stew.
7. Patrick put a plastic cowboy in the cupboard, against Omri's wishes.
8. Omri points out that Patrick would have a hard time hiding the cowboy from his family.
9. Patrick says that unless Omri brings the cowboy to school, he will tell about the little men.

Chapters 9-10
1. When the cowboy sees the gigantic Omri, he thinks that he is having a hallucination from drinking too much alcohol.
2. Omri wants to keep the cowboy away from the Indian; a knothole has been shoved out of the crate.
3. The cowboy has been trying to shoot him; Little Bear is angry with all white men for taking Indian land.
4. The cowboy cries easily, so he is nicknamed "Boo-hoo."
5. He wants Little Bear to help choose a wife.
6. Omri places Boone next to Little Bear on the seed tray and puts the food between them.
7. egg and beans

8. Boone says that the food smells good, but both complain about having to eat together.
9. Answers will vary. Omri is prepared to part them if they get too rough; maybe he figures they will get the desire to fight each other out of their systems

Chapters 11-12
1. The water is for bathing; only Little Bear wants to bathe.
2. Adiel has lost his shorts; their mother has discovered that Gillon didn't finish his homework; the father can't garden because it is raining.
3. He doesn't want to get into a big fight while he is holding Little Bear and Boone.
4. Little Bear is bored and does it to get Omri's attention.
5. Omri lets out a yelp while the headmaster is talking.
6. Little Bear asks for company.
7. Patrick demands loudly to have them both.
8. Patrick has been in the music room trying to feed the little men. Miss Hilton sends Omri and Patrick to the headmaster's office.
9. Patrick is giggling almost hysterically from the strain of having such a wonderful secret.

Chapters 13-14
1. Patrick wants to prove to the headmaster that he isn't lying.
2. Little Bear is from a time in history before Boone's.
3. Omri tells the teacher that he drew the tiny drawing because he wants to have fun with the teacher—to see the teacher's amazement.
4. He rejects one in a yellow dress and one in a blue dress, but approves one in a red dress.
5. Mr. Yapp sees the cowboy and Indian and thinks Omri has stolen them. Patrick vouches for him and when Mr. Yapp is allowed a brief look at what is in Omri's hand, sees that the figures are indeed like the ones Patrick described as Omri's.
6. Adiel thinks that Omri has taken his shorts, but Patrick finds the shorts behind the radiator.
7. They are looking for the key.
8. Little Bear has gotten stirred up by watching pioneers shoot Indians on a TV western; Boone has been cheering on the pioneers.
9. Little Bear mutters that he is sorry, sobs, gives up his chief's cloak to cover Boone, calls the spirits in dance to let Boone live, offers to go under the floor-boards to find the key.

Chapters 15-16
1. They take turns sitting up with Boone, who is badly injured.
2. They know that the rat is loose.
3. It suddenly comes to him that the key must have dropped under the boards in his room when his father opened them up while looking for the rat.
4. He doesn't know about the rat, but would probably go even if he did.
5. Tommy plunges a tiny hypodermic needle into Boone's chest, stitches up the wound, and gives Little Bear minuscule iron pills to administer to Boone.

6. Boone starts talking about the "redskins" in the movie.
7. He doesn't want her to see him and grow frightened, but he wants to watch her reaction to Little Bear.
8. Boone fakes a faint and asks for whiskey.
9. They have a brotherhood ceremony. They feast on nuts, chips, chocolate, tiny hamburgers, bread, cookies, cake, soda. After Boone's and Little Bear's wrists are nicked, Bright eyes binds their wrists together. Omri and Little Bear also become blood brothers.
10. Answers will vary. Omri realizes that the little people belong in their own time and that it would be disastrous to keep them in his. The boys leave the cupboard empty "just in case."

Activity #5: 1-stability; 2-longhouse; 3-commando; 4-tantalizing; 5-compost; 6-escarpment; 7-pommel; 8-unwarily; 9-uncompromisingly; 10-foreboding

Activity #6: Set #1-parka; Set #2-maize; Set #3-tomahawk; Set #4-galvanized; Set #5-magnanimously

Activity #7: 1-L; 2-I; 3-T; 4-E; 5-B; 6-A; 7-R; 8-S; 9-D; 10-O; 11-M (LITTLE BEAR STABBED OMRI)

Activity #8: 1-bewildered, unconfused; 2-boundless, limited; 3-pitilessly, kindly; 4-mesmerized, bored; 5-minuscule, immense; 6-uproar, lull; 7-impatient, relaxed; 8-dazed, alert; 9-meat-eating, vegetarian; 10-soiled, immaculate; 11-diminished, grew

Crossword Puzzle solution appears on page 44.

Comprehension Quiz, Level 1
1-F (The cabinet was a present from Omri's brother, Gillon.) 2-F (Omri was not thrilled by the plastic Indian his friend Patrick gave him.) 3-T; 4-F (Only the plastic ones became real.) 5-F (Little Bear protested that he wanted a longhouse, not a tepee.) 6-T; 7-T; 8-F (Omri wanted the knight's ax for Little Bear.) 9-F (The old chief died, possibly of fright.) 10-F (Omri's father didn't press Omri about what he had done with the seed tray, but insisted that it be replaced.) 11-F (Omri kept the secret from his brothers.)12-F (Little Bear used the paints to put Iroquois signs on the tepee.) 13-T; 14-T; 15-F (Omri, who brought the men to school after Patrick insisted, was careful to keep them hidden.) 16-G; 17-A; 18-B; 19-E; 20-F

Comprehension Quiz, Level 2
Completion: (Accept variations on wording.) 1-cupboard; 2-Indian; 3-great-grandmother; 4-the toy Indian has become real; 5-longhouse; 6-WW I medic; 7-knight; 8-old chief; 9-ax; 10-headdress; 11-dies; 12-he is chief now; 13-cowboy; 14-bring the men to school; 15-tell the secret

Short Answer: 16-Only plastic items became real in the cupboard.

17- He ties some of his own hair to a twig; Omri gives him the mug from an Action Man toy; Omri cuts a small piece from his sweater.

18- Patrick is impulsive, thinking of his own pleasure, unlike Omri, who worries about the men's feelings.

19- He wants to keep the wonderful secret to himself and also worries about what his brothers and parents would do if they knew.

20- Little Bear stabs Omri and Boone shoots Patrick; both little men are frightened when they first see the "giants."

Novel Test, Level 1
Identification: 1-D; 2-E; 3-B; 4-A; 5-I; 6-G; 7-H; 8-F; 9-C.
Multiple Choice: 10-C; 11-D; 12-A; 13-D; 14-B ; 15-B; 16-A; 17-C; 18-B; 19-D; 20-D; 21-A; 22-B; 23-C; 24-B; 25-C; 26-D; 27-C; 28-A; 29-D; 30-B; 31-D; 32-A; 33-A; 34-B; 35-C; 36-D; 37-C; 38-C; 39-B; 40-B

Novel Test, Level 2
Identification:

A. Omri is the main character of the story, a boy who discovers that he can make plastic toys real by locking them in his magic cupboard.

B. Patrick is Omri's best friend. When Omri tells him the secret of the cupboard, he insists on putting a plastic cowboy inside.

C. Gillon is Omri's brother, the one who gives him the cupboard as a birthday present.

D. Omri's father is a man who likes to garden. He respects his sons' need for privacy.

E. Omri's mother is kind and tolerant, entrusting him with the key her grandmother had given her.

F. Little Bear is an Iroquois Indian who comes to life in the cupboard.

G. Tommy is a WW I medic who is brought to life, tends Little Bear's wounds, and is sent back to the war.

H. Boone is a cowboy who cries easily. When Patrick brings him to life, he doesn't get along at first with Little Bear.

I. Adiel, Omri's oldest brother, gives him a helmet for his birthday.

Short Answer:
10-13: Answers will vary.

14- Patrick threatened to tell the secret of the cupboard, otherwise; Omri could have refused to bring the men and waited to see what Patrick would do, or sent the men back to their own time in the cupboard.

15- Answers will vary—Omri thought that the friendship would be over if he didn't.

16- Patrick, who had been in the music room trying to feed the men, got in trouble for being late to class; Omri got in trouble for talking to him.

17- Little Bear enjoyed painting the symbols on the tepee and Boone told Omri he enjoyed drawing, then drew his hometown.

18- They started arguing while watching a violent western and Little Bear shot Boone with an arrow.

19- Little Bear climbed under the floorboards and had to dodge a pet rat; he was trying to find the key to the cupboard so that Tommy could be brought to life to help Boone.

Essay

I. A. Omri might think about the morning he first saw Little Bear, problems they solved together, the brotherhood ceremony.

B. Students should retell part of the story from the little person's point of view. Boone, for instance, might explain that he thought he was hallucinating when he first saw Omri and Patrick's faces.

II. A. Students who choose to answer A should mention that Omri has become more mature, aware of others' feelings. He has learned about the Iroquois way of life—and how much responsibility it is to have someone's life in your care.

B. Essays should include the fact that both are schoolboys who sometimes get into trouble with teachers; both are inventive, used to like playing with plastic toys; Patrick is more impulsive than Omri, less likely to think of the little men's feelings, more likely to blurt out secrets, use threats to get what he wants.

III. Essays might refer to these pros and cons:

A. pro-Omri's brothers would probably want their own little people; con-Maybe Omri's parents could have kept the secret and helped solve some of the problems Omri ran into.

B. pro-Omri might have prevented the injuries to the little people, the death of the chief, the problems at school if he had refused to use the cupboard's magic; con-Omri would never have made friends with Little Bear, Boone, and Tommy, if he had refused to use the power of the cupboard.

IV. Personal essays will vary.

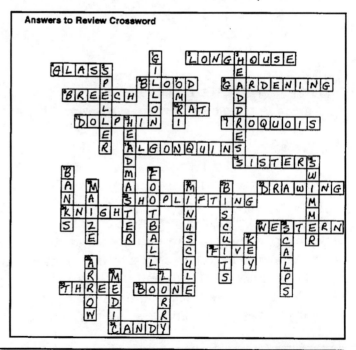

Answers to Review Crossword

44